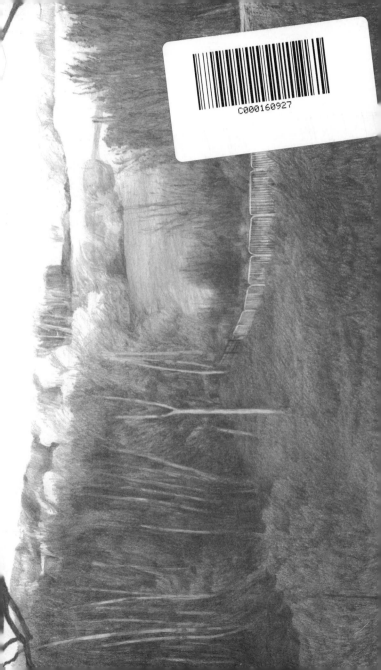

"With a ruthless rush of witty adroit prose Collings whisks us in his series of short stories through the madness of human eccentricity. Not for the faint hearted, the light hearted or even the young at heart – in fact it's better if you don't have a heart at all."

John Healy – author of *The Grass Arena*

"The Myth Of Brilliant Summers is the work of a powerful writer who insists on taking risks with language and structure. Austin Collings writes prose that is compressed, angled, droll, sure, but also evocative and swooping when he wants it to be. These stories are so tight they have an elegance of form that somehow does not jar against the rough, darkling content."

Daniel Woodrell – author of *Winter's Bone* and *Tomato Red*

"A stream of haunting images, familiar but not tired, illuminate powerful descriptions of noble ordinariness. Collings has a mastery of his language, relationships and environment. Authenticity ripples through every sentence. The working class have a new literary hero."

Kevin Mitchell – *The Observer* and *The Guardian*

"This impressive collection is a breath of fetid air. Collings' characters seem to come of age and then carry on careening through a world gone horribly wrong. Their summers may not have been brilliant but his prose certainly is: staccato bursts infused with energy, punches to the gut of society's artifice, low, low blows. Austin knows where the bodies are buried. And now so do you."

Larry "Ratso" Sloman, co-author of *Mike Tyson's Undisputed Truth* and *Scar Tissue*

"Forget bogus pessimism, this is real pessimism like mother used to make. Austin Collings says 'no' in a thousand inventive ways. Good on him."

Ian Pattison – novelist and creator of *Rab C. Nesbitt*

"Austin Collings writes some of the best new stories I've read in ages. Cutting to the very heart of what matters, his terse prose forces us to take a good hard look at the world about us and at ourselves. This is frontline reporting from Britain's city streets. Truly powerful and uncompromising. Collings is a major new talent that deserves to be read and celebrated. A very fine collection."

Ron Butlin – Scottish Poet Laureate (2008–2014), and author of *The Sound of My Voice*

"These terse and haunting stories from the decayed heart of England are percussive and unforgettable. A truly impressive collection."

Howard Cunnell – author of *Sea On Fire* and *Marine Boy*

"'Summer days, when things go wrong,' is the opening to one of the stories in Austin Collings' collection, *The Myth of Brilliant Summers*, but it could just as well be true of all of them. Young lads muck about together in the holidays, but they're not engaged in the Blytonesque plunging into pools and riding ponies that the title suggests. These lads watch pigs being slaughtered, see a man and woman engage in a very public fight, get texts from blokes who've been in the nuthouse. Their world is urban and harsh, encapsulated in graphic prose whose cynicism rolls back to reveal clear-sighted observation and ultimately, compassion."

Jean Rafferty – author of *Myra, Beyond Saddleworth*

• The Myth of Brilliant Summers •

Austin Collings

P
A
R
I
A
H

The Myth of Brilliant Summers
Copyright Austin Collings 2014
ALL RIGHTS RESERVED

Published by PARIAH PRESS 2014

PARIAH PRESS
www.pariahpress.com
pariah@pariahpress.com

British Library Cataloguing in Publication Data
Collings, Austin
The Myth Of Brilliant Summers

ISBN 978-0-9930378-0-1 paperback

Illustrations by Chloe Steele
www.chloesteele.com

Photography by Jonny Walsh © 2012 – 2014

Cover art by Steven Cherry
www.designstevencherry.com

Set in Monotype Dante
Typesetting by Bracketpress

Printed by CPI Group (UK) Ltd.

· Contents ·

• Illustrations •

· Images ·

Note to reader: This book is designed to be read on the bus or in the pub before or after they've tried to slowly kill you again at school or in work or even at home.

All the characters and places herein were once real.

• The Uncertainty of Subways •

Look closely at our Biro blue, melancholy mornings; our sinister pink summer nights; the sweep of seasons; skinny trees stood like malevolent pitchforks on quiet street corners; windows and net curtains, and the decades of bile and love hidden within. Something has changed. The once familiar has become distorted. The allure of absence is at play. I wander down a mystery of streets. No more *the regular*. Tarnished by experience, the spaces are now loaded with all manner of associations: the threat of the unseen; the uncertainty of subways; unfathomable solitude.

Instinct tells me that things could go wrong here. The death vibe. Kids could stray, or go missing or get lost at a time when the curtains had ceased to twitch. Girls could lose their virginity amid the rank quiet of the empty, wet woods. Leadless dogs could sniff out all sorts in the mean chill of the morning: their long toenails cracking through frozen leaves. Sullied experience seems to infect the air in what could easily be viewed as a pervert's paradise. It could all happen, or already be happening.

And always, at the corner of things, here in the edgelands, the scrublands, or Dog Shit Valley as some people call it, the darkness wants in, like the pleasant devil in Dennis Potter's *Brimstone and Treacle*. There's something else there too, lodged at the back of my mind; a predatory back-story that haunts the landscape, that sounds like a bark – like a dog barking to itself, angry with itself – telling me, all the time, that the balance of nature is an illusion.

· Tommy V ·
(Crimes Against Nature)

He had all the makings of a man who could injure innocence. Rumour had it he'd once played for Man Utd in the Seventies; rumour also had it he liked luring teenage girls into his small flat with the promise of powerful, cheap cider and small, but much-needed, sums of money that could change their lives for a week or so; until they'd spent it all on coarse make-up or coarse cigarettes or coarse boyfriends who never thought much of them in the first place.

His name did the rounds at school. He had fans. Girls' lips seemed infected with it. They talked about spending time with him, up in his flat, near Red Bank field. He'd gladly go to the off-licence for them. *White Lightning, Hooch, Vodka, Embassy Red, Embassy Blue, L&B* ... If they didn't have enough, if they were a bit short, he'd make it up, pull the required coins from his rank pants, and satisfy their needs. All nonchalant. All *no problem*. This was his unique power: his timing, his cunning generosity. The good feeling he gave you. Few could match it.

One night they watched Pink Floyd's *The Wall*. Some of them got stoned. *Comfortably numb*. Other men's names would be mentioned as well. One lived above an ironmonger's shop, near the canal. He was much younger than Tommy. Early 20's. The beginnings of a moustache. Weed-inspired eyes. Short, shaved jet-black gel-bright hair: little more than bristle, or head stubble, barley hair even. A military buzz-cut. Girls would go and see him at dinnertime, share chips and cigs and then come back into class smelling *like fag-ash*, as one teacher described the whiff. But mainly they talked about Tommy V and the things he gave them. The times they had together. I'd see him every now and again, shuffling around, with his weathered granny trolley wheeling through glistening puddles, road reservoirs and mushy leaves the burnt shade of brick; his complexly creased skin like well-done bacon, yellowy eyes on the verge of curdled milk; wafting his signature whiff of damp indoors. Airing himself. Biding time before night. Before the girls come round. He was a mystery to me. He had a pull that intrigued me. He gave me terrible, frustrated night's sleep, mulling the mystery over, fixated by his ways. I wanted what had become his: the company of Lyndsey or Joanne or Mandy or Juliette. A companion to guide me through the teenage wastelands. The frustration made me feel

4

weary, as if I was locked in the early days of a cold, my head bunged up. He came to signify all that was habitually wrong in my hometown. Not that he was much different than any other aimless man that existed on my local estate. Young, old, some-where in-between, few of us had anywhere special to go, and most men were all small town wanderers in their own way – my dad included. This wasn't what singled Tommy out. He did that himself, with twisted passion. A legend in his own pint, it was he who spread the rumours and spat the lies into people's ears: the Man Utd connection, his strong Manchester-Irish connections … And then he'd *let slip*: "We just sit up and talk. If they want to stay over then they stay over. Their choice. They're not completely underage. We're not talking kiddies. They know their own minds … better than most. I just help them out from time to time." And the girls continued to enter his flat and receive his gifts – those tiny tokens of affection that never failed to win them over, and sometimes draw a smile. Their pleasure seemed genuine. Some felt chosen. Selected. Small stars among their limited peers, the other girls: the unchosen. He had them in his pocket. How did they not see the things I saw in this man so clearly: his rotten potential, his seedy skills? In my jealous, teenage eyes, his kindness was meant to confuse and manipulate, and he appeared to be getting away with some kind of murder: toying with, and disrupting the process of growing, of becoming; giving it an adult-spin, all of his own making. Only, the girls didn't seem to mind it happening. They played their role well. The visits continued. And weirdly, Tommy became one of them. One of the gang. And maybe it was this simple truth that I couldn't fathom, that lodged in my system like an unopened conker; seeing them gathered in ragged unison, on the corner, across the road from the quiet bungalows, obsessing over cigs, their bright laughter concealing excited nerves, as they wait for their provider, their old friend, to turn the key in the door, to let them in.

· George & Dragon ·

I'm trying to discover a murder that never happened. I wanted to write a book about it, but that didn't come off, didn't work out as I would have liked. Problems with money and all that. Bad timing. I can't help feeling it would have helped me in some way, helped me shed this weight of discovery – of wanting to discover a murder. It's ever since I saw that frozen image of her on the North West News: her old, pasty, fog-coloured face. That turquoise jacket. Bright orange background. Photo booth stuff. I'm guessing it was her bus pass picture. Overuse would have crinkled it, if she'd had the time to overuse. Instead she was found dead in the bus station toilets. First thing in the morning. The night before she'd stopped off at the George & Dragon pub in Bury after visiting her daughter in hospital. The hours in between were *crucial*. Took the police 12 years to find *their* killer. A former soldier.

The Scientology Organisation have given
37,000 members Psychic Powers and
Committed Genocide upon 7000,000,000
Human Beings.
They control children with beams and spells.
Crying over someone who died on a cross.
Christians are victims.
I went to Heaven and found it to be tardy.
All written and disseminated
By L Ron Hubbard - The Devil and Anti - Christ and
You can do anything you want to a non
Scientologist.-L Ron Hubbard.
Scientologists sign 10,000,000,000 year contracts -
with Satan Hubbard.
Psychiatrists label him as a psychotic - a paranoid
With a construct of hatred, He detests bodies -
Homo sap, sentient vegetables, Meat bodies.
Psyhiatrists label him as a psychotic - manic
depression.
Scientolgists see animals as their 5th impulse
to survive, God as their 8th impulse to survive
And ethics as their 9th impulse to survive.
Scientology staff, receive £90.00 per week
from housing benefits.
The Scientology Organisation have a 4000 strong
uniformed army - all with psychic powers.

· Off By Heart ·

I hear her bra-strap snap. Her bones crack. The sound of her age.

• Wits End •

In the evenings something comes over me. His words hitting home: one after a–bastard-nother.

"I've no option but to let you go ..."

His uneven teeth, like war-torn buildings.

"I can only apologise ..."

Professionally indifferent. Cold to my rent. Cold to my needs. A cold man in a small oveny room, backlit by afternoon sun: transformed by light.

" ... "

All of a sudden it gets calm. We have nothing more to say to each other. We will no longer walk the same carpet.

Tonight, God is in hiding.

I now have to learn the world all over again.

· Night Fishing ·

She took me to see her dad one warm afternoon, though we had yet to have sex or see each other in a truly hungover state. On the way there, in her cramped car, she told me that he was once a feted jazz drummer who lit rooms up but he was also a heavy gambler, hard drinker, hard liver, and now he's in a wheelchair.

I can't remember how he'd ended up disabled, not exactly. It happens to me a lot; people tell me all manner of things and I'll retain most of it, effortlessly. But sometimes, on the rare occasion, I'll be told something serious or important or crucial – like a name, or a set of directions, or the reasons for her dad's immobility, as in this instance – and I'll have no recall of it whatsoever. Not a jot.

He lived at the bottom (naturally) of a housing block and his arms were abnormally small (this had something to do with his affliction) and his voice, whiny. I stared at him and thought about other musicians with disabilities: how they cope etc.

She asked him if the kids had been round to see him. She wanted me to hear this conversation. I could tell. She wanted me to know that the kids liked him because he didn't see himself as an old bloke in a wheelchair but still as the twentysomething – and thirty and forty-something – havoc-wreaker. He didn't care about them smoking spliffs or drinking, and they liked to ask his advice – this eternal tearaway in the wheelchair. That was his role. They looked out for him and he did the same for them, in his own way.

He smiled with delicious delight as each of his own, well-chosen, well-rehearsed words wobbled in the air. He had it down pat, the whole routine.

"Are you still night-fishing?" she asked him.

He and a few others – kids and stray (male) adults – would head out at night and go fishing in the canal. The cans would pile up beside the wall, not a drop left in them.

One night a new man arrived, but he'd had a *real skinfull* and fell in and they had to pull him out. A few of the older lot, who'd been fishing like this for some time, became anxious about his presence, more so when it happened again the following night. He unnerved them. They were on edge, on pins, whenever he turned up, waiting for him to hit the point where he drifted towards the water: the drop. Together, they decided to tie him to a pole with a rope, like they do with dogs outside shops. Her dad said he looked like a big wrinkly toddler on reins. But the rope did the trick, saved him from an ignoble end.

Soon after, her dad started tying himself to the steering wheel of his van using *strong* Sellotape. He wasn't supposed to drive, in his condition. But the tape worked wonders and it was his decision, his life – was it not?

· Colourful Language ·

My dad was fond of using the phrase *colourful language* whenever he talked about work, about lifting bricks in the punishing sun, or climbing a ladder, soused in rain ... *'You hear all sorts on the site. A lot of colourful language ...'* He'd talk like this, intimate and reflective, whenever we walked to the library at night. He said it was a *mug's game* – the *game* he was in: the building trade. He told me not to end up like him.

· Because We Are Also
What We Remember ·

The pull of the bus station: its damaged air drew
me in. Whenever I'd walk past the Ladies, near the
café where they served milky coffee with a resilient
leathery skin on top, I'd try to imagine her final
December night. The moment of murder. Mum,
dad, or a mate; didn't matter who I was listening
to – or appeared to be listening to; the real conversation went on inside, and was purely interior.
Consumed by wild imaginings, vivid projections,
the scenes flowed like a dark lake – brutal brain-
clips that made a mockery of my teenage wisdom.
They induced an odd euphoria, an addictive urge.
I saw *all sorts*. My normal, mainstream concentration – the one they wanted me to use for school
and home – suffered. I found it hard to come back
from that other place. The dark lake. The mark
had been made. The impression set. Soon after, I
started to imagine things that never happened;
deaths that were never on the cards. The final
breath of teachers and kids.

· Uncle Frank ·
(Jackpot)

Saturday afternoons in Jackpot with Uncle Frank and his missing finger; my 7 year-old-eyes curiously dazzled by the colours and symbols of the various fruit machines. Uncle Frank elevating himself, telling lies about himself, identifying with Tony Montana in *Scarface*, talking out of his arse non-stop about Tony Montana's white suit: how if he was to buy a suit, then he'd buy one very similar to that one, that white one, very similar to the one Tony Montana wears in *Scarface*.

I wander off; leave Uncle Frank pestering the wiry Pakistani sat behind the thick plastic protection screen that muffles words. Soundtracked by the childish, giddy whizz-bang sounds of the fruit machines, I go on a short tour. Three in the afternoon, and it's dead. Unpeopled. No dropped coins, clanking.

I'm drawn in by the fruit graphics and the BAR sign and the speed of the spin, but I haven't got a penny on me to feed them, to load their greedy guts. No use asking Frank. He's not that sort of uncle. He's ungenerous; makes a big deal, high drama about giving you the odd 50p, the rare pound. On the odd occasion when he does give, the coin – or coins – are handed over slowly for the purpose of those in the room – there has to be other people in the room – to see it being handed over, as evidence.

I spend the remainder of the afternoon, staring, focusing back and forth between the machines that I'm desperate to play, and Frank, noisily fingering coins in his pocket, stood at the front of the 'shop', dreaming out loud, confidently fibbing, believing every single word he utters; too real is the feeling of make-believe … A barrage of incidents; everything happening to him, all the time. Non-stop. No let-up. You wouldn't believe it, but he does believe it. The Pakistani nodding and blowing out cig smoke and keeping tabs on the door, on who's coming in. But nobody comes in.

Even now, years down the line, he still lives in this fantasy zone, still weaves elaborate stories to people just wanting to get on with their day. Already his recent tall tale of (canine) heroism is falling apart at the seams. Contrary to what he'd originally told people, he wears no sign of week-old stitches on his hands: the dog – the bullmastiff – didn't actually attack him as he'd originally said, but went for his own, much smaller, furry friend.

How he actually managed to kill the dog has yet to be fully cleared up. It may forever remain a mystery like other chunks of his unusual life. All we know is what he tells us, that he strangled it somehow, with it's own collar in the middle of the street, in daylight – broad daylight. Silenced this terraced terror, this frothing beast, twisted it's collar tight … The hero. The vigilante. Or so he tells us.

· Patterns ·

Lie down and listen to the sound of children
screaming at dinnertime. Soon the bell will ring
and their small bodies will be filed in an *orderly
fashion*. Led back into place. The quiet classroom
bright with sun. This brief lull of silence will be
routinely interrupted with the sound of a dog in
anguish. Desperate for somebody to let it back in.
The distress rising in it's *voice* as time nears 3, or 4,
or 5. The innocent hours. Meanwhile, planes dot
the sky and fly on obliviously, nosing through thin
chalk-like cloud marks: creating a unique wind
noise. I picture a giant, *breathing out*. The big king
of everything. And maybe the occasional siren will
sound too. My ears are tuned to all of these
changes. The comings and goings. Barricaded
within brick, little surprises me. I have lost a lot. I
don't mind. There's always more.

· Why must I be a teenager in love? ·

Come the pink nights of summer, he'll lay her down amongst discarded crisp packets, stones and stony mud.

Beneath him, she'll turn her head away and while thinking this isn't right: him, her, the vroom of cars, unseen, from afar; strands of her hair become tangled inside an earring.

The school day after, she'll not be doing what she should be; thinking, instead, about him and last night; the bruised bags below his intent eyes; his age. The silence after.

Come 3.30pm, away from the dusky corridors that change children, and squeak, the giddy crowd of kids can't disguise his waiting car, outside the gates; nor his thin, pale gingery arm goosebumped by the breeze through the open window. Later he asks: 'What took you?'

· The Dying Bite ·

The cold steel swing frame: green, like the railings, corporation green and steadily weathered. Both flake easily.

With cold hands, I stop picking and touch hers; also cold, from holding swing chains that rattle, like something more sinister.

Near eight, the near night can't hide the angry pink of her nail polish, applied yesterday but now also flaking.

And I don't know why, but something about those nails, their inelegance, is inevitable.

• All The Sad Young Men of All Ages •

There are cracks in the walls of the Job Club: prominent black sores on the ceiling and vein-like lines stemming from the skirting boards. And somewhere unseen the radio blasts out dated dance tracks. Techno traces from my youth; some sort of airwave haunting.

A father and his son sign in at the makeshift reception desk. The father doesn't look well; looks fearfully thin, like a yellow skeleton or a gaunt dog; and the son's ears are partly scabbed over. I felt a skew-whiff sense of sorry for them; as if I was in any way different, as if I didn't share their small prospects and daily defeats.

In silence, we each sit on bright blue swivel chairs, around a cheap newly-polished (you can smell the sheen) gleaming (false-wood) wooden table. Five males. And a female inquisitor who doesn't miss a beat as she asks, after introducing herself: '…and what do you do?' I confidently reply, 'writer', and not so confidently follow it up with – 'But I sometimes work other jobs: temping and whatnot ... '

As the others tell their stories, a genuine part of me told myself – seemed to whisper to myself – that none of this was happening: that the sanity of daylight would intervene and I'd find myself somewhere less demoralising. Back in the room I struggled to rent, staring out of the window, at rooftops and TV pylons: waiting for who-knows-what, again.

Tensely holding his hot plastic cup of black coffee, the father smiled at me politely. I nodded back at him, and then looking away, concentrated on the design of my fingers – glared at the permanent new moon shape at the base of my fingernails.

Seated in front of a computer, we were told to fill-in a questionnaire. One of the questions asked: *Do you sometimes get angry with your work colleagues?*

As the rain continued to mark and darken the windows, smudging our view of the outside with messy splatters and gloops – shapes that only water can make – I look over at the son's computer screen, as he waits quietly, with dignified patience, for it to register his carefully chosen answers, and predict his 'top' occupation. His face doesn't flicker as he reads the words: Abattoir Assistant.

· The Myth of Brilliant Summers ·

Pete's dad limited himself to four cans of Skol. Every night. Take the dog for a walk. Come back to four cans of Skol. Every night. The house smelling of potato-hash. Potato-hash clinging to the furniture, their clothes, their whole being: the whole family. And the dog.

Summer, dying again outside as we waited for Pete, inside, with his dad and those unopened cans: a small, nasty part of him resenting our muted teenage presence. Every night.

The headlocks he got us in as the budgerigar screamed in the background resonate with age. He held us tightly; forced us to fight it; to fight his own sinewy strength. A point was being proved. But the point was lost on me. I just didn't want to be near his small unpredictable body, didn't want to be stared at by his eager, ratty eyes.

His odd anger was unfathomable. The aftermath, even more incredulous, as he'd sit back in his tatty chair, and open the first can, with a dangerous smile playing across his un-handsome face. Every night. One summer.

· The New Grunts ·

I'm seeing more and more soldiers in town, recruiting. Each day, I turn the corner, round the bend,
near the old Ritz cinema that occasionally plays
genuine classics, and there they are, with their black
recruiting van, their (mis) informative leaflets;
stocky lads and men, posture all military stiff and
upright; shirt sleeves rolled up like John Wayne or
Robert Duvall, revealing thick arms, each of them
squinting in the piss-coloured sun, waiting for a
new candidate. One more recruit.

I watch them eyeing up the edgily excited girls
milling around outside Argos and Al's Fried
Chicken. The girls are what we used to call scallies
but now they call chav. It'll be a different name in
the future but the undercurrent will remain nasty
and diminishing. That's the way it goes. That's the
way we've been brought up.

I don't like the soldiers – or squaddies, as I prefer
to call them. At school only the unhinged showed
any enthusiasm for such a strict and limiting life.

I preferred to stare out of windows. But look where that's got me: skint, wandering the Merseyway by day, and worried awake at night, picking through the bones of my solo limelight.

I've never bought into the hero rubbish either; the idea that they're actually *saving* me. I may need saving, but not in the way they go about it. And I don't like their records, their sentimental cover versions; the whole charity aspect; or the overly emotive public that buy them, and pride themselves on wayward grief for people they don't – and never will – know.

They used to call them grunts in Vietnam. Young lads from poor backgrounds; brainwashed by the lies of privileged men. Blown to fuck in foreign fields.

I walk past them, amazed that it keeps on happening. And then I walk past Waterstones and there in the window is a book display centred on the Falklands War. I'm not feeling much with the way my life's going; mostly I'm numb but aware. Yet, this display digs deep; plummets in my gut, and merges with a heavy sense of scalp-tingling annoyance – as if I didn't know the answer to a simple test question; as if I was doomed. And I'd like to

text somebody or ring somebody; to tell them it's
happening all over again. And when will it stop?

· Taxidermy ·

It glared back at me from all corners: on buses;
front page of the local paper. In the deep peace
of the library it lay strewn and tattered on the
entrance floor. That picture of her. The complete
stillness of it seemed more startling than any
violent action. Nobody came forward.

· Home Brew ·

She was a thickset woman with a strong sense of her own importance. Soon after she moved in, over the road, with her scruffy husband and quiet daughter, she got talking to my mum. She told her she was a nurse. She worked nights, sometimes. You could see the bottom of a white uniform beneath the oversized coat she always wore. She had no reason to lie.

Later, we found out she worked in an old people's home. Her husband stayed at home, making home brew. The daughter went to the same primary school as me and my sister. Everyday, taking herself to school, head down, spellbound by kerb and gutter, rarely looking up. But sometimes the occasional glimpse revealed itself when the sun shone and she was forced to lift her face and squint, to register this invasion of light that impinged upon her shadowy mask of fringe. Even her eyes were silent.

Before the husband pulled a knife on my dad and

brother, the wife had told my mum that she *took things* from the patients. *Only little things, mind.* My mum said you could smell the home brew on her breath as she'd told her this, one morning.

After the knife incident, my dad floored the husband on a Sunday afternoon as we walked to the corner shop. Shock altered his face as he hit the deck. Holding onto the front gate outside somebody's house, he supported himself back into position, into his usual upright, imperfectly vertical self. His long, lank and unkempt hair, hung from his head like a new limb. Pushing these oily strands away with nervous fingers, he looked at the pair of us, all mock innocent, taken aback by this swift turn of events, as if to say *there was no need for that.*

Later on, a skinny Hispanic-looking man with a permanent oily tan moved in with them. He brought his young daughter. They'd met him in the pub one night – in the Lord Rag'. I'd sometimes see him loitering around the small shopping precinct, outside Kwik Save, and the indoor market, dressed in his signature green leather jacket, pointy black leather shoes, always smoking, his daughter nowhere to be seen.

· Mystery of the Half Nelson ·

We'd call each other names as we walked the summer streets, feigning purpose, on the lookout for incident, or action. The names became a bad habit that we each shared. A common tic. We couldn't free ourselves from conflict. Our lashing out derived from powerlessness; they say that's the case, the more powerless one feels, the more one is likely to lash out.

A galaxy of spots warred with one of our faces: enflamed it, like a day-old pizza. Caramel-coloured teeth affected another. Somebody's pants fell short, revealing a shock of white sock. We called this *cats-died*. One of the more unfortunate among us had a long, hook-shaped, distinctively disproportionate medieval nose and flat tarmac-like hair that gleamed with grease. We were not blessed. All of our features seemed to continuously – and relentlessly – let us down.

Dictated by confusion, permanently low on spends, we couldn't fathom the advantages of staying in or going out. Creeping inertia tingled in our scalps like black electric wired beneath our ungovernable skin. Once out, on the streets, thoughts shifted quickly to being back in, off the streets. Undecided, adrift in uncertainty, we became highly-strung.

There seemed to be no release, no real answers. The course was set. The road, part-travelled. Tight-lipped, we each shared the doom, like sullied prisoners entwined into a secret code.

Then when the nights began to draw in, we'd knock on strangers' doors and leg it, run off and hide behind clapped-out garages, or inside ginnels, not saying a word, tense smiles stitched excitedly across our small faces, full of thrill and the curiously warped joy of wrongdoing.

The door rush soon died off, never to be mentioned again: one more unspoken part of our fractured friendship. And days passed into days with dreadful certainty, as if they were on repeat; but we were not old enough to change the channel.

Repeating ourselves, today a déjà vu of yesterday, we went back to see what we'd already seen before, to walk the same summer streets again. Never giving up. Doing our best to make it better, to alter the course. Up and down concrete hills, beneath mute trees, past crackling traffic and unpeopled bus stops and glowing chippies, our shady reflections in parked car windows, moving from one to the next … On and on, the days bled into one another, like a pile of undiscovered dead soldiers.

We had no time at all but it seemed like we had forever, following girls, plucking up *the courage* … But *the courage* appeared to do us little good. You can't live on hope and wishes. So we continued to demean each other with names. Pick holes. Gradually, it became an addiction. We knew no different. And always, we made our way home separately, alone, through the deserts of certain suburbs.

• Mother Brandy for Sorry Jon •

Jon sent me a text just before Christmas. He said he was doing fine, drinking brandy, watching TV with his mum at home. He's not been so good lately. Bouts of madness. In the summer, he rang me up and told me about these signals. Dark signals. He *had* to smash up the TV. He'd got so frightened he couldn't go out and get a 10-pack of cigs from Tesco's. It got that bad.

But the text seemed a little less dark. Not that he was out of the woods. Maybe he'd never be out of the woods. But there was hope there, in that text, I think – or I'd like to think. Then again, he's on that couch, in that unkempt living room most day of most days. His mum upstairs, not too good herself. Unable.

When we last spoke he was determined to get back out there, playing the drums. With shaky enthusiasm, he read me a review from an obscure American jazz magazine. His voice sounded *shot*. Nervous. Trademark *sorry* whenever he lost his way, or thought he'd lost me, on the other end of the phone.

They'd got it, you see; the mag writers, the jazz aficionados from across the water. They understood what he, and his two other group members, were up to – what they were trying to get at – locked in their tiny rehearsal room over the road from Strangeways Prison. The effort and toil. The love. And it mattered to him. He was holding onto this review for all it was worth. He wanted to get back there, back playing like that.

I didn't say that I'd heard the review before, when I last saw him; the same afternoon I brought round a new (second-hand) TV for him to sit in front of, each day. He'd read it to me then, only with an even shakier voice, because he'd not long since got out of the nuthouse.

"Try and not destroy it this time, Jon." I said to him as he searched for a clean cup in the chaotic kitchen, directly beneath his sleeping mum, upstairs.

• Carpeted With Feathers •

Up on the makeshift farm, they'd sometimes crowd around to watch pigs beaten to a vivid end with clubs. Material dropping out of their caved-in heads, like beans dribbled from an opened can. *You can imagine the noise* … My brother saw them at it, one day in the six-week holidays: teenage-lad-eyes deep in different forms of concentration, some repulsed, some revelling, as that high-pitched pain squeal – *the noise* – seemed to adopt a shape in the summer air: a terrible arc. The clubee was the father of my brother's best friend. They came from a big family. He radiated presence. His force was visible. Hands like shovels. Mirror image of a 1950s B-movie actor who stands up to dinosaurs. Prone to flying off the handle. Next door were no strangers to his raised voice, his *moments*. With the pigs clubbed clinically, dropped like sacked spuds on pre-blood-stained paving stones, the lads turned their backs to the breathless bodies, slumped in death, side by side, leaving the dad to gawp and mull over his next move, soaking up the sunny quiet after the violence, as in *the now* as one could ever be, peering down at the *slain swine*, chin nailed to his large T-shirted chest, eyes squinting at their brutalised facial features, their big ears, pulped; the only movement, his thick rough-as-brick fingers groping for the gold Benson & Hedges box in his pale-jeans pocket. *Where does one go from here?* Connected (to some degree) in shock – or various states of shock: high, low, complex combination of both – the lads made their way towards the hot shop down the road with the hard-to-open door in need of instant repair or instant replacing. No air getting in. Chocolate bars, sweltering inside. Fridge, not warm as such, but certainly not as it should be: sour-smelling; milk, on the turn. Owner, behind the counter, sweat-wet, staring with seasoned suspicion, jerkily alert, and far too obviously unsure about these clumps of kids who have just unstiffened and clattered through the door, entered noisily, *fucking-this* and *fucking-that* and giggling, with no sign of letting-up. Immediately, shiftily, they roam the three small but well-stocked aisles; so quick and so *teenage*. His eyes enlarge and blink not once as he watches them with enormous concentration. He cannot hide the feeling that kids like this worry him. *Pigs* get mentioned as they find their prey. The cold relief of the opened freezer, head dipped in, picking out the right lolly or choc-ice. Temporal bliss. One of them farts and they all laugh as the farter denies farting. The counter-man's serious face de-volumes their laughter and they pay in sullen silence, leaving back out beyond the stiff barrier, struggling with it's crappy hinges, out into the pre-afternoon sun, where they'll stay for as long as they can, trying to prolong time. Many years later, local residents reported a leak – or something like a leak – that seemed to be flowing from the farm: chicken blood, trickling down the residential road, temporarily marking the kerbs near the church and the graveyard, swilling into the public drains. The local news described him as a 'small producer', owner of an 'illegal slaughterhouse', who sold meats to friends and families to make 'soups and stews with' – and the floors of the slaughterhouse were 'carpeted with feathers'.

· The Gist ·

Paleing away, pressed like a flower, becoming
nobody. I see examples of this everyday. Abstrac-
tions of memories. Body and ground merging, as
darkness tells the time. This is the gist of it. Our
comeuppance.

· Parade ·

Close-up like this I see his skin has more in common with red leather than wrinkles. He's riveting to look at that, like the cracks in a painting are riveting to look at; the way they draw your eyes in, beyond the actual image you should be seeing, into the surface chaos, the tears of time.

He inserts a cassette into a paint-spattered radio. An ominous, dark, brooding sound enters the clammy atmosphere of his one-bedroom flat.

"Black Sabbath ..." He says, mumbling along to the warbled lyrics as if I wasn't there: *"People say I'm heavy, they don't know what I hide ..."*

His unsteady, vice-ridden hand reaches for the volume control. Louder, it sounds even more chaotically distorted, tattered and tuneless, and not quite right: as if there was something wrong inside the machine – a hidden malfunction.

"Do you want a bit on this?"

Jittery, misshapen, kipper-coloured fingers hold out the small remains of a joint, still visibly damp at one end.

"I'm alright Tommy…"

He turns the music down a bit.

"Nothing wrong with that. More for me."

I can still hear faint traces of it playing in the background. An eerie murmur. A scary-sounding nursery rhyme. Pulling on the bitter end of his joint dimp, he squints as he inhales, creasing his face into the contorted shape of chewed chewing gum. Then, turning his face even more wrinkly and maroon, he hacks out a cough that rocks him forward from his seating position on the battered sofa.

"A bit harsh that. It can burn terrible sometimes, if you're not careful."

I said nothing as I walked to the window at the end of the room, looking out at the empty football field at the back.

"There'll be a night game soon," he says, staring at

the turned-off TV, his face still marooned by that coughing fit. "I like night games."

In the opposite direction I see a set of long-derelict garages illuminated in melancholy, lamp-lit orange, and close by invisible drunks can be heard arguing the toss over the distant sound of a train, pulsing through the night.

"I'm always hearing that train but I never see it." He says. "Wait there."

Done staring at the blank TV, up off the chair, joint still clamped in his thin lips, he enters the bedroom, coughing, phlegming up, orchestrating a gravelly sound, as if his insides were made of rubble or broken stone. After a minute or so, eyes watering, wiping spittle from his chapped lips, he returns with a large ASDA bag full of books, their pointy corners straining the plastic, escaping their confines.

"I remember reading this one when I worked in Prestwich Mental Hospital. Years ago. You wouldn't even have been born."

He held up a copy of *The Shining* by Stephen King. The cover was the same as the film poster. I knew this because my brother had the poster on his side of our shared bedroom. Jack Nicholson's vile eyes, Shelley Duvall's gaping fright. Their faces and expressions occasionally unsettled me as I tried to fall asleep.

He dipped back into the bag, rummaged around, placed a handful of Polaroids carefully to one side, and threw me a copy of *Jaws*. I picked it up off the pond scum green carpet. This also had the same cover as the film poster. It felt damp and sodden and some of the pages were wilted, shaped like waves.

"That's much better than the film. That'll fucking shit you up: the descriptions ..."

His palpable enthusiasm forced me into a nervous reply: "I've never read it."

I didn't want him to lend it to me. I didn't want the hassle of not reading it, and then the hassle of having to return it pretending I'd read it.

"You should. They didn't know what they were doing with the film. I read that when I was working at the hospital too. You had a lot of quiet nights in there. Odd like that. You wouldn't think it. A mental hospital. Quiet. But you didn't want to let it get to you. Start thinking all-sorts. All sorts of nonsense. Drive you fucking potty. It's a fine line when you come to think of it."

He continued digging in that plastic bag.

"And this ..."

He held up a damp, twisted, out-of-shape porno magazine called *Parade*. Beneath large yellow lettering, a woman with conker-coloured hair in blue underwear grinned a seedily innocent smile. I couldn't take my eyes off her.

Miniature flecks of hot ash fell from his joint onto her face and breasts, quietly sizzling as they bled through the front cover.

"Dropping bombers on it – on her."

He flicked the ash – the joint sparks – onto the carpet, where they mingled with other marks of neglect.

"Lend it ... I've seen enough of her anyway. I'm sick to the back teeth of her. I've seen all of them in there. I know every page *like that*. To tell the truth.

If I'm honest."

Flashing a doggish grin, he started chuckling, then coughing. Coughing himself inside out, he looked spent: emptied.

"Take it. I've got loads more. Bags. E-ya …"

Wincing with cough pain, he picked the magazine off the floor and held it out, staring at me with full-fat milky eyes. A silent plea / offering. A moment shared. Then I heard his can coming to an emptily tinny end. The dregs. He dropped the magazine back onto the carpet. The moment had passed. His enthusiasm had passed. I looked at her face, at her body, her blue underwear, lying there, crumpled, next to Jack Nicholson, beneath the living room table that needed a clean. How long had he kept her here, up on the fourth floor, above small hordes of other lonely men? Tommy's A4 girlfriend.

· The Stuff of Paint ·

Amid the deceptive ordinariness of the paintings, he'd throw in an intensely detailed pencil drawing of Billy Casper flicking the V's, or a serious Ian Curtis pulling on a cig, or a serene Peter Sutcliffe wearing a bow tie. Later on I read that he was one of those lads who'd absorbed the world view of older men – his dad in particular and that he'd spent his youth listening to The Fall, The Specials and The Smiths – sarky bastards with an edge and a motive that wasn't solely related to the mechanics of music. The connections made sense. In secondary school he was the Caravaggio of the canteen who drew shiny pots and kettles and naked women from *Penthouse* that looked just like shiny pots and kettles and naked women from *Penthouse*. The dead spit. Naturally, he was bullied by older lads who wore pin-badges with names that carried their own confrontational physicality: 'The Clash' and 'The Buzzcocks'. He couldn't distance himself from these youth-clips, these scenes from *the passion*; they controlled his body clock. *Will the chip ever fall from our shoulders?* Later in life he'd wallow in the comfort of pub-time, looking clever, composing notes, refining his tastes and obsessions. Serial-killers' handwriting. More Seven than West. Inky scribbles that taper off and fragment after the fourth or the fifth pint of Guinness: the black doctor. The trail: always leading back to one place. The back of beyond. Then there's the detail of the actual paintings – their sombre force. The goal posts, the labour clubs, rinsed-out skies the colour of prison porridge, schoolyards and hopelessly frayed garages with knackered doors or no doors at all; empty of cars or any discernible purpose. Mausoleums to a shared past, now on its last legs. Our eyes have seen it all. I breathe in the paint. The clock that underpins these delicately menacing stills is neither here nor there, suspended somewhere between a before, and an after; almost as if Nic Roeg has been given God's hands for an afternoon and nobody knows how to re-edit his final cut. Time's arrow: up the swanny. Mundane meltdown. No more Bourbon biscuits. No more Stella. No more heartburn. The last sounds have been heard and I'm guessing it wasn't the final blast of The Beatles *Day in the Life* but something more readily disposable and fitting to this everyday end-scene: a crap swan-song like Zoë's *Sunshine on a Rainy Day* blown into the sky above the old school, near ASDA. Then no more. No sound at all. The last silence.

COVENTRY CITY

STEVE OGRIZOVIC

· The Remedial Block ·

Here was a place that took cases that no one else would touch. The window-lickers. The spazzes. The spaccas. The thick as shit. The unhinged. The badly-made. All would be seated in the small blue block that stood on small black steel ankles, near the canteen, in front of the large grassy space where we played intense games of football among ourselves at first-break and then later at dinnertime. The remedial lot seemed to have their own clock, their own structure. We didn't mix. They were cut off. In the summer, sun hit the windows, knifing shards of English light across our eyes as we tried to concentrate on the flight and whereabouts of the trusted casey. A dazzling blindness. Those inside the small blue block must have felt bullied by the warmth. It's close creeping attention wrapped around them like a kidnapper's unwanted cuddle. No way out. And then when rain fell, and died-off, gently, the windows fogged up like breathy specs, and you couldn't make out who – or what – was inside. Our peering revealed no clues. A reflective mystery. Did the remedial lot even exist? As the weather grew worse football time became something else; a one-room, interior drama, once called wet-play, but now given the different, slightly less childish, more corporate title: indoor break. With the rain faintly tap-tapping outside, and somehow also tap-tapping inside of us, flicking at our skulls with frustrating precision, incessantly reminding us what we were all missing out on, our outdoor privileges – our daily airing – we turned to the small blue block and it's mysterious inhabitants. Perfect fodder for our taboo-less tastes. Lets take shots at the cheap shots. Whenever we probed and asked, the teachers looked curiously found-out, guilty-as-they-come and innocent. We'd hit a raw nerve. Naturally, we wanted to hit it more. Hit it harder. Ugly spirits need feeding. And though we each shared a common nothing, the teachers and us – no great plans, no concrete future to speak of, no other life to walk into, or inherit, or inhabit, or feel confident about – they refused to let us in on this one, to open up about the small blue block. The hidden truth remained hidden – well hidden. Gradually, some of us saw the weak and disabled, the slow-to-grasp and slow-to-fathom, the *unseen-needy*, as threats, or like a sting in the forehead. The shots got cheaper. Anger swelled. This act of superficial rebellion, of brash inquiry, brought us closer together. Friends are not for escape. They are for conspiracy. All the while, outside, strings of rain hung around, getting in the way, like a bad dream curtain you can't quite walk through to get on stage and start doing your thing. Fleetingly, a weak sun would appear, fluttering like inept animation, and with it, fat black flies resting on splintered window frames. And though the sight of it – those brief slices of washed-out-yellow light – lifted us from the dumps for a short while, we knew the inevitable had set in again for another year: summer had had it's day. The cold was coming.

· Tether ·

My dad nodded at me as he came out of the toilet, followed by the loud sound of flushed waste.

"I said 'Morning'," he said.
He hadn't *said* morning; he'd *nodded*.
"Morning." I said.

Tension entered my gut. Hollow nausea. I waited on the landing until he went into the bedroom. The smell of shaving foam toured my nostrils as he passed me. Downstairs my mum banged cupboards. I wondered how many times I'd been in this position – Saturday morning, staring down the shaded staircase, my dad in the bedroom, preparing to get out of the house, my mum downstairs, pissed off. I wanted him to know that I didn't hate him, that it was a different day and last night's argument with mum was a relic now, never to be unearthed. But I didn't know where to start. He had a way of making me feel guilty for what he'd done. Yet, I felt protective towards him; away from the building site, in the thick of his problems, again;

the debts; his frazzled wife – our frazzled mum; us ungrateful kids. How he must love being in that pub, or that betting shop: away from it all for the time being. The sanctuary. But, as always, I said nothing, just walked into the bathroom, and took stock of the mouldy walls, the frosted window flaked with a generation of rain, the band of building site grime that constantly encircled the bath, the beige gunge that keeps building up at the base of the taps.

· Mothlight ·

The off-white, skull-coloured, wrinkled wallpaper. The naked light bulb. Moth dancing on the 60 watt. Afternoon racing on. Volumeless. A summer afternoon quickly descending into the partial darkness of early winter P. M. Sudden shade. Tommy V, sat on his epically worn settee, mutely open-mouthed, immersed in some festering kind of silence. The noises outside – kid calls, the odd siren, spade chinking concrete, a distant bass-boom, distorted ice-cream nursery rhyme, kid cry, kid laugh, mum shout, rag and bone man's garbled language bordering on gibberish and sounding both full-whack and yet far far away, dog bark like an amplified cough, mate of Tommy's shouting *Tommy*, then, once more with feeling: *Tommy…You in?* All of these noises seem to have been made by, or originated from a different life-form than Tommy; sat there, slowly sweating, encaged in the close, cloying, muggy warmth of a pre-storm afternoon, having *difficulty unwinding*, trying not to grind his grey teeth and doing his best to think of nothing at all.

· Pinned Hopes ·

I watched as she sat enraptured by his TV presence.
Her eyes gleamed, fervently, as he shook public
hand after public hand. The personal touch goes
far in politics: the power of pressed flesh.

*"We are on the side of ordinary people against privilege,
against vested interests of the public or private sector."*

Again, the weather was beaming. He seemed to be
permanently bathed in brightness or lit with a last-
ing glow: his own personal sun. And then there was
that smile: that hard-to-forget, hard-to-dislodge,
positive, uplifting and beatific smile, revealing all
those teeth – so many teeth.

*"I can't stand politicians who wear God on their
sleeves."*

He made her happy, made her forget herself briefly,
forget the mum-life. This was glory time and she
wasn't alone here. He made a lot of people feel
this way, feel the fickle euphoria of forgetfulness.

Immediate nostalgia; that's what he'd mastered, that's what he conjured and mustered; this towering figure of middle-class certainty.

"We are not the masters now. The people are the masters."

A nation primed to be spellbound, in awe of euphoric make-believe. His vast and compelling hold appeared incorruptible. He appeared to have found a lucky way to live. His lies and suave treachery were not yet apparent of course, at this critical stage – how could they be? And the far-reaching barbarism that defined *his spell*; this was not yet envisioned, realised or even imagined. Not back then, in sunny glory time, before *the smile* was seen differently.

• Human Ash •
(The Dissolve)

With our raw red eyes locked in, and our peripher-
als playing tricks, inserting lunar spears and black
acne and tiny be-jewelled 50p coins into our *field
of vision*, we lay down in the tall tickly grass,
lonely stoners stoned on cheap weed, *taking in* the
glamorous pink sky, marooned in personal worship
to the explosive line of bright yellow laced through
this brilliant canvas, severing it like a messy news-
paper rip that seems to control the hand – and
not vice-versa – the net-less nets in the not-so-far-
but-could-be-miles-away distance, a shirtless lad on
a loud crosser bike, tyreing up dirt-dust, bouncing
through the gates of the goal-posts with the
focused ferocity of an apocalyptic Sci-Fi hero
fleeing a mad mob of mad bastards, time getting
on for 7, maybe later, 8-ish, all with a lot on our 16
year old minds, so much clutter and unluck to look
back on and rake up, so much threat, so much TV,
so many albums of noise and melody that gave rise
to emotional notions of escape and success, ambi-
tions beyond the rational, so many film scenes cut

into our keen eyes, indelibly embedded now, for reasons of pleasure and kicks and simple survival, *we all draw on our heroes*, so many girls lips unkissed, though the thought had never – at any stage – passed their lips, *grave mistakes*, unrewarded efforts, *fears of annihilation,* school rooms, and dread rooms, and the vermillion mist of the nowafter, here splayed out on the grassy deck like big skint skin flowers, potential carcasses, hypnotised by sky, amazed by the thing, but to utter a word at this moment, would kill the moment, stone-dead, de-pulse the drama of watching, in mute alignment, this warm otherwordly light, each of us individu-ally coffined almost, in deep thought, some kind of absorbed weightlessness, where lonely energies come together; yet, as in life, the moment must also kick-the-bucket at some stage, and so it will, soon; but for now, for my own sake, imagine where the weed would take me if I closed my eyes, and exited this particular frame of mind, to go from one to the other, from the dim pink of this delicately beautiful night, with the wind picking up, ghosting, whispering, *dust seems to be eternal*, to – what an unusual glow, darkness …

· The Winds ·

This one night we heard sobbing outside. Then the words: "You talk about me like I'm dead." Followed by a female: "I don't recognise you when you're like this." Then silence. I looked at my girlfriend, sat on the edge of the bed, shiny as a balloon after her late-night bath. *"The wind..."* She said, staring at the dark beyond the open window, hypnotised by the cold entering the room.

• The Blackbird of Paradise •

Reduced to mute by the distortions of memory – something about the balance of his mind being *disturbed* – he'd wrapped her in carpet and taped up the door using duct tape. When I hear this it's as if I'm hearing a chorus of voices but I don't know what they mean. See, we never get told that we all die in our own arms.

· Orders from Chaos ·

Traipsing home over the decaying ruins of the old bombsite, the sad perfume of cut grass floats before me. I have the distinct and eerie feeling there might be somebody down there, still clinging on: not beyond rescue – not completely. An almost-corpse: 9/10ths dead. I'd like to screw this morbid thought into a crumpled ball, ditch it somewhere, walk away. Not let it set in. Further on, in clear view, a *staff* dog with a mouthful of tennis-ball runs towards me, as if it was the devil's very own instrument of torture, pounding the defenceless landscape, flattening small blades of grass into clawed mush. It's bright excitable eyes speaking volumes – deafening volumes – of potential terror. Called to order by it's young owner, I'm relieved to see it slow down slightly, temper it's predatory litheness as it drops the now piss-wet ball onto the ground, casually adopting a stance of icy civility. Dead calm. And all at once, the glow of the park seems misplaced. It's heavy warmth suffocates, pinning me to a standstill. A tense hang nail-like ssshhh descends. The future has become the present. The air tingles with non-movement, with the creeping static of what-next? The horror of contact. I think about moving forward, closer to the source – to get a closer look – to remain faithful to the moment. To serve time's wishes. Allow the love of the good ghosts to make it all right.

· River Street ·
(Polaroid)

Summer days like this, when things go wrong
beneath rooftops that cut the sky. Mesmerised
by sun on brick, I recall it all like a familiar 1980s
Polaroid. Everything off-centre. A last flicker. The
bloke with the 'tache and the white shirt tucked
into tight black pants, cleaning his car, listening
to Ellie Goulding *Anything Could Happen*, could
be from any age. He looks timeless, in an acutely
dated way. The hoover has been dragged to stretch-
ing point and inside his house I see an uncluttered
hallway leading to a slice of kitchen, aglow with
what-could-be, but obviously isn't, angled mirrors.
I walk past his (black pant/black sock/black shoe)
leg, hanging out of the car. The noises don't
register – not completely anyway – until I turn the
corner, away from the furious din of the howling
hoover and a loud Goulding, *letting darkness grow*.
A well-tanned women, with hair pulled back tight,
flat and tight, like Karloff's Dracula, faces up to
her boyfriend or husband, who holds one hand
down the front of his see-through white tracksuit
bottoms.

"I said get out of my face."
"I'm not in your face."
"I said get out of my face."
"I'm-not-in-your-face."

On the other side of the road, two teenage girls stand outside a run-down Asian phone shop/newsagents, enthralled by the goings-on. Biting her bottom lip, suppressing a gleeful smile, while widening her eyes, the smaller of the two girls holds this (maybe put-on) look of excitement for the duration of the exchange. The other girl absorbs it all with creepy stillness: blankly intense; dead-eyed, deadpan, dead unimpressed. Seen it all. Upstairs, above the shop, face hovering at the small window, an Asian man can be seen peering out from behind curtains the colour of dried blood, and a time-spoiled 'To Let' sign, eagerly attentive, wholly engrossed like the kid at Christmas who looks – in all the sense of the word – with fierce determined passion, projecting presents in the toy shop window into his own hereafter. He sees it. Beyond the bare reality of looking. Four lads stuffed into a fast car flash by, giddily beeping the horn. The arguees continue their schizophrenic dispute. *I'm not in your face.* The problem of identity: of not being somebody other. Problems that won't go away. Not ever. Ends never meeting.

The crux of love. Will battles. Brain drains. Clots of anger. Many pains. The ordinary, ceaseless din of it all. More Northrot, on River Street. *Just don't. I'm telling you now. Just don't. Don't give me that.* You get the feeling they know exactly where they're going with all of this, that they've been here many times before, *at each other's throats,* treating the street, the shops, like a big house, like their own big house, forcing the issue until that critical moment when one of their faces wilts and dampens in exhausted, effortful defeat. The stress-heads. It's intense, but routine, and I don't think it's going to get physical. I don't think he'll hit her, or she'll hit him, or any of that. I think they'll just go on like this for the next few minutes, measuring each other's limits and thresholds, knowing when to pull back just before one of them snaps. Nearing them, I feel involved. Connected. My heart quickens with questionable excitement. All about to pass them, I catch a closer glimpse of the man. He's built young, but looks old. A lot of people look this way round here. They grow old, young. Tired teary eyes, filming over. Thinning on top. Bald patches. Skin like pensioners' fingers. Emotionally pale. Voice strained, like that of a loyal smoker. Words like weak coughs. A palsied expression. *What? Tell me what it is?* The quarrel melts as I walk further away. Perhaps it gets clearer elsewhere.

· August Britain ·

Releasing a dreamy drunken piss at the urinal, a
thickset builder decked out in an a dirty dayglow
Hi Viz jacket sidles up next to me. After theatrically
unzipping, he drains a steaming waterfall. Like a
high-rise suicide, it drops tall and spreads messy. I
stare forward, focus on the scarred wall; the
chipped plaster, and wait for him to zip up. Emit-
ting a long, heavy blast of breath, he mutters some
garbled darkness to himself about stupid fucking
dogs, being sick in the head, yawns noisily and
crashes back into the body of the near-empty pub.
I couldn't tell whether he knew I was there or not.
Not washing my hands, I exit the toilet, palm the
creaky door open. Cher's on the jukebox, asking:
'Do you believe in life after love?' I finger through
a rats-nest of clammy fivers and hand the diminu-
tive female pensioner some money in return for a
pint of golden fizz. The days pass over me and I do
nothing. Keep coming back here, to this place, this
non-event. David Cameron appears on the TV in
the corner of the room. I look up to watch his
mouth shape volumeless words. Beneath the telly,

a young skeletal lad with pale grey skin sits, asking his much-older and less-drunk drinking partner: 'Can you tell a snake from a garden hose? But can you?'

· Web ·

Bad dreams of offices; of wheezing computers,
low-ceilings, stark lighting, carpet; and how I
belong to that place like a chair, or an envelope; and
not as the boy who once looked out of windows
with a smile.

· Bob ·

Downstairs he screams as Bob slices further into his ear. *Be Here Now* is then turned up louder: Noel Gallagher's *Magic Pie* increased in volume, filling the kitchen, muffling the man-wail slightly. Unable to listen anymore, I get up out of bed and quietly, stealthily, leave, out the front door, into a Saturday-2am dark, where I wander for long minutes, waiting impatiently for Bob and his mate-enemy to be done, knife acts all finished, for sleep to take over the house.

Desperate, I make my way round the back, peer over the fence, kid myself that it's stopped; music, muted; Bob finished operating, finished slicing through the back of his ear with a kitchen knife; but there they were, two large shapes in the kitchen, sat at the table, legs dressed in tracksuit bottoms, feet in trainers, upper halves in unzipped coats; two large shapes wired beyond reason on local-cut-cocaine and canned Red Stripe and Fosters, talking loudly over one another, but not shouting; their thumping voices leaking from the lit window. I stop peering, take stock and think all sorts of tired and defeatist thoughts. My life really had come to this, exiled from my bedroom by Bob and his plum-skinned associate.

The morning after, the house is quiet and dark. The kitchen, damaged; knife marks in the wall, slits and dents and scrapes and coins of blood dropped all over, dried to a compelling red, smeared across the table, beneath bent and folded cans; a myriad of images ignited, lingering in the head like an odd presence on a street corner. That indoor scream of his: the howling. Me, wandering the streets, pining to be back in bed, encased in the red glow of sheets, dozing off my own drink urges. Each thought entangled and made more worrisome by lack of sleep and a hangover: what end would all this damage lead to?

Days later I'm told they went to the pub together the following afternoon: necked a load of pints and several vodka-Red Bulls, chased down with more local lines: the blood now dried a crusty dark red behind his 1/10th severed ear; the knives back in the cupboard; *Be Here Now* still spinning in the CD player, twirling silently, volume turned right down. Barely a word spoken about the previous night. Other things to talk about.

· Meantime ·

I buy a pint and sit down in the beer garden.

In my youth I used to think my detachment gave me superiority over the others. Now I just see it as detachment.

One twenty-something lad wearing a frayed hand-me-down-style check shirt talks with a cultured stutter about his role in the world: his unstoppable success. His much-older (all male) audience of two agree with him, tell him he's right – *'you're right … spot-on'*. I tell myself he's the boss – the young boss – and that they're working for him, and that's the only reason they're agreeing like that, with such intensely focused glee. I could be wrong.

In the near corner, shaded slightly by the wings of trees, I notice a woman sat among a small crowd of four. Her phone starts ringing. Speaking into the Blackberry that fills her faintly wrinkled, but still sleek and well-groomed hand, her face *turns serious*; the transformation so quick as to be almost violent

– or similar to the onset of violence – to the *turning point*.

Then it eases off, this explosive expression of hers, switches, becomes something else altogether; a picture of punctured desolation; a lonesome gaze; as if she's being forced – by who-knows-what or who – to watch her own funeral. She remains on the phone, but she doesn't speak.

Right on cue, the sun's disorientating glare intensifies. The shade clears from beneath the trees. Blotches play havoc in front of my eyes. A baby starts wailing, as if it's on fire; as if it's swallowed too much sun. The lad in the check shirt laugh-speaks the words, *'fuck yeah dude...'* and then, with dreadful urgency, the woman raises her well-mannered voice into the Blackberry; because something's wrong – I'm hearing something go wrong. I can tell. Just tell. Anxiety is the fastest drug, and you can just feel it. Some sort of graphic mayhem, or negative mania is playing out here.

We never notice anything do we? Not until it's happened. Not until we can look back with concern – or what we think is concern, but may well just be the motions; or even pointless politeness.

We're simply not designed to understand the moment.

And then she asks: *"Do you remember what it was that you said?"*

· The Collector of Foreskins ·

He claimed to be the second son of God. Beneath
his once-cream washed-to-thin shirt, a bra could be
seen gripping his thick flesh like wire, splitting his
back in two. Part *this*, part *that*. The line of divison.
He smelled of mince.

· Yellow Grass ·

There's a painful prettiness about the day, about the summer pulse of life itself. Trains gift me all kinds of sights. Yellow grass and wet windows that dry quickly with speed. I could stay here for some time I think. Remain in motion, twisting my neck occasionally to look at her, sat next to me – her green eyes. For a moment it seemed as if this is where colour began.

Natalie Curtis © 2014

Austin Collings was born in 1980: the year of the monkey. His work has featured in *Sight & Sound*, *The Times*, *The Guardian* and *Tate Etc.* amongst other publications. He co-wrote *Renegade: The Lives & Tales of Mark E. Smith* published by Penguin. He currently lives in Manchester.

• A Word On The Words •

The Myth Of Brilliant Summers is typeset in Dante; originally designed in the 1950s as a metal letterpress font with the intention of imprint into, rather than onto, the page. Its history remains entwined in the lives of Pariahs such as Alighieri, Griffo and Boccaccio, and includes a style that was heavily influenced by the developments of 15th century Venetian punchcutters.

Dante; keep it infernal.